D1637957

Lucy's Blue Day

My Diary

Chris & Lisa Duke

Copyright © 2019 Lucy's Blue Day Ltd.

All rights reserved.

ISBN: 9781085941334

DEDICATION

For Our Girls

CONTENTS

ACKNOWLEDGMENTS

Chris & Lisa would like to thank the following people for their help in creating and continuing Lucy's Blue Day.

Fred & Lesley Higgins
Federica Bartolini
Andrew Price & all at Astute

Every school, every workplace and every person we have visited since this campaign began.

"LUCY PEAR HAS WONDERFUL HAIR IT CHANGES COLOUR LIKE NO OTHER."

ALL ABOUT ME

Hiya,

I'm Lucy.   You might already know about me and my wonderful hair.   Well, I say wonderful, but do you think you would like it if people knew how you felt ALL the time?

My hair is strange and not a lot of people have it – it changes colour...I know, right?

My natural hair colour is yellow...blonde, whatever you want to call it.   It's that colour when things are fine, nothing is wrong and I'm not particularly excited or happy...just fine.   It's yellow most of the time.

When I get angry, my hair goes red and I mean really, REALLY red - not the red-headed red like my Dad (I like his hair) but as red as a bus or a postbox! Like BRIGHT red! If you see my red hair, you know that something, or someone (usually Brad), has made me angry.

Things that make me angry:

- If I hear someone talking about me behind my back
- If I hear someone talking about one of my friends behind their back
- Bullying
- Homework at the weekend
- Brad
- Brad
- BRAD!!!!!!

Brad is my little brother, and the most annoying person in the world EVER!!!

BRAD IF YOU ARE READING THIS...PUT IT DOWN
NOW OR I'M TELLING MUM!!!!

He keeps me up at night. He wakes me up early in
the morning. He's messy, smelly and a BOY!!! He
annoys me ALL THE TIME!!! He is either sticking his
tongue out at me or he's making faces behind mum
and dad's back, kicking me under the table, stealing
my phone and uploading videos of me dancing on
social media or texting my friends things that I
100% would never say!!! EVER!!!! He is just ALWAYS
THERE and makes me mad all the time!!!!

My hair is going red just thinking about him now.
The good thing is though, when mum and dad see
my hair turn red out of nowhere, they know that
Brad has done something, they just need to find
out what...

Sometimes, I get jealous, not often but it does
happen. When that happens, my hair goes green.
Yellow hair I can live with, it's my natural colour,
even red hair doesn't make people stare as much
but when my hair is GREEN...people look!!! I don't

like being jealous, I don't like feeling it. It's not a nice feeling but when someone gets something that I have wanted for a long, long, LONG time, I feel jealous and the green hair is on show.

Things that make me jealous:

- Alyssa, one of my besties, got a new phone
- Summer's house
- BRAD!!! Sometimes Brad gets things when I don't, and I get jealous.

I remember the day I first woke up and my hair was purple, it was my 6th birthday. I woke mum and dad up at 6:30 in the morning...I was soooooooooooo excited!! I didn't even care that my hair was purple, because it was my birthday, it was the best day ever and I got lots and lots and lots of presents.

It's not all about the presents though, it's just when I am happy and excited about anything, my hair goes purple. You know how I said before when my hair goes green, people look? When it's purple, I don't care that people look. It's great! I love my purple hair and my mum and dad love it too because they know I'm happy.

Things that make me happy & excited:

- My birthday
- Christmas
- Family trips (yes, even with Brad...sometimes)
- Hanging out with my friends
- Roller-skating
- Being on my scooter
- Holidays

And so much more!!!

There is another colour that happened to me recently. A colour I have never felt before or even seen. This is the reason why I'm inviting you to read through my diary. I want you to understand how I felt that day and what happened throughout it.

Believe me, not everyone gets to read my diary (BRAD...OUT!!!!) but if it is going to help you, and other people, understand about these feelings, then I am willing to let you. But please, promise me that you won't let Brad read it! And not just any old promise, I need you to Pinky Promise!

OFFICIAL CONTRACT

I _____ on _____ and
(my name)   (date)

forever more will **NEVER EVER EVER!!** show

Lucy's diary to her little shot-nosed

fart-breath twerp of a brother BRAD and I

mean **NEVER EVER!** No matter **WHAT!**

Even if he offers me 1 trillion pounds

I will still NEVER show this to him

Signed _____ Date _____
(my name)

— Thank you —
Your friend
♡ ~ Lucy Pear

"WHEN THE SUN SHINES BRIGHT AND THINGS SEEM RIGHT HER HAIR IS AS YELLOW AS THAT BIG BRIGHT LIGHT"

Date: 14th September
Hair colour: Yellow

Do you remember a couple of weeks ago when I wrote how excited I was about going back to school and my hair was purple? I was so excited about seeing all my classmates, my friends and even my teachers. It was amazing! I was literally SO excited! So happy to go back!

Well, it's been two weeks now and it's just a bit meh...nothing special at all. Don't get me wrong, I ~~love~~ LIKE school. It's fun...sometimes but nothing really exciting or interesting has happened. It's all been...okay.

The best time I had so far was when Mrs Higgins, my ~~favrite~~ fave teacher, was in a great mood. She brought in sweets, she put music on in the classroom, opened the windows so it was nice and cool and let us sit anywhere so long as we got our work done. Everyone just had an epic day!! I like Mrs Higgins, she's a fun teacher!

When I woke up today, I knew it was going to be just another normal day. I can tell what kind of day I'm going to have when I check my hair colour in the morning. If I wake up with red hair then I know I am going to be angry ALL DAY so it's best to stay away from me for that day. That wasn't the case with today. My hair was yellow.

I had my usual breakfast, sat in my usual seat on the bus and got into school at the usual time.

Lunch time I sat, as usual, with Alyssa & Summer - my BFFS in the whole wide world. They are awesome and I love them. I sit with them almost every day and we talk and laugh and have fun. I like normal days when everything is right.

A new boy started school today too. He's very quiet and always had his hood up so we couldn't really see him very well.

After school, I came home to find Brad in my room! He's SUCH a little fart-breath! He was playing on my tablet again - watching videos online. It is so annoying when he does that because I can never find what I want to watch through all of his silly "opening-toys" videos. I mean, seriously, who actually wants to watch a video of a kid opening a "Surprise Egg"?!

I yelled at Brad to get out of my room, told him that if he didn't leave, I was telling mum. He didn't even look up from the screen, didn't even respond to me...Ugh! He makes me so mad. I yelled, again "Brad, put my tablet down and GET OUT OF MY ROOM!!!" He turned around to look at me with a smug look on his face but his face changed right away...he then said "sorry", put my tablet down and left - he's so weird!

The rest of the day was pretty normal. We had pizza for dinner, watched TV, played on my tablet

and went to bed, ready for, probably, another normal day tomorrow.

I like days like today. I'm happy, and

nothing is strange. My hair is a "normal" colour,

and no one bothers me with how I feel because yellow/blonde, whatever it is, means I am happy and today...I am happy.

Goodnight xxx

I can't sleep. Why did Brad look at me like that? It was very strange. He's so weird but normally he just keeps going until I tell on him. Maybe he wants something from mum or dad has promised him a toy? Maybe he just wants to be good from now on. HAHAHAHAHAHAHA! No. That can't be it.

"WHEN LUCY IS EXCITED
FULL OF HAPPINESS AND GLEE
HER HAIR GOES BRIGHT PURPLE
FOR EVERYONE TO SEE"

Date: 21st December
Hair Colour: Purple

OMG! OMG! OMG! OMG! OMG! OMG!

It is actually only 4 days until Christmas!

I LOVE CHRISTMAS!!!

I love everything about it! The songs, the decorations, the people, the PRESENTS!! I love that Christmassy feeling.

It's the weekend, so my dad took me and Brad into town to get some presents. I love walking down the main street hearing all the people chatter with excitement, seeing all the Christmas lights sparkle above me. I love feeling the cold air on my face but, strangely, it makes my nose itch. I wonder if anyone else gets an itchy nose when it's cold too?

Dad took us all to get some
hot chocolate - probably
one of my favourite things
to do. Hot chocolate just
feels so….Christmassy!
There's nothing better
than drinking some hot
chocolate with
marshmallows that have
melted inside and
whipped cream on top

when it's freezing cold outside. I like holding onto
the mug to heat up my hands. It helps my nose
stop itching too because I like the steam heating
up my face.

We sat in the warm coffee shop. Dad likes a
window seat so he can "people watch". I never
fully understood what he meant by that until this
year.

Outside on the darkening street which was lit up
by festive lights, twinkling lights, sparkling lights

and the biggest Christmas tree you've ever seen in your whole entire life right in the middle of the town square, I started watching the people walk by. Some were really flustered-looking - I bet they forgot to get someone a present. Other families were swinging their kids while the kid jumped and even over the noise of the people outside, the clinking and clanking of the coffee cups in the shop and the people chatting inside, I could hear the kid shout, "wheee! Again....1...2...3...wheee!" and then giggling away. I could see people holding hands while they walked with bags of gifts in their other hands.

Even though I could see their breaths because of how cold it was, and their cheeks and noses were red, they were still smiling. I love looking at the different scarfs people wear. This one girl had a rainbow-coloured one, well, kind of rainbow-coloured: it was missing orange and pink, but it was really nice.

I now understood why my Dad liked to people watch. It was really nice to see so many happy people around us.

The Christmas Tree was amazing this year! It was so much bigger. I remember Mum saying about something she'd read on her phone. Something about the town saying their Christmas tree would be the biggest it's ever been. It definitely was! It had a huge silver star on top. Last year it was an angel. I like the angel, but I like the star much better. It lit up so much of the sky!

Just as we were finishing off our drinks, carollers started to line up in front of the tree. I could see the conductor organising them into position and I asked Dad if we could go and listen. He said YES!!!! WOOHOO!! We finished our drinks and went over and stood among the large crowd of people that had gathered in front of the singers and waited. All of a sudden, they started to sing "Silent Night". It's my favourite Christmas song! I don't know why but I love it and it makes me feel really nice and calm inside. Dad put his hand on mine and Brad's shoulders and squeezed them really gently. It was really nice. Brad gave Dad a hug after as well. He does have a heart then...

We stood there for their whole performance. It was nice to have that time with Dad and Brad, even though we didn't say anything - we sang along to "Rudolph the Red-Nose Reindeer" and "When Santa Got Stuck Up the Chimney" (this is Brad's favourite!) but in terms of speaking, we didn't actually say anything.

When they finished, Dad asked us if we needed to get anything else. We hadn't bought mum anything so we asked if we could go and get her something. We went into a jewellery store and Dad bought her a bracelet with charms on it. Mum's been saying she wanted a charm bracelet for ages, so Dad said he'd get some charms from us to add to it. I think he got a heart, a ring and two smaller hearts that were joined together. I assume they're meant to represent me and Brad, but I don't know. I just know Mum will absolutely LOVE it!

We went back home after that and I realised that Brad and I didn't fight all day - not even once. Not even a little, tiny argument. Nothing. I really liked it actually. It would be nice if he could be like that all the time. He told me his New Year's resolution/Christmas present is to be nicer to me and to not read my diary anymore. This would be the BEST present from him like EVER!!!

Although it would be nice if he got me something I could open - you can't unwrap kindness and I got him something he can open so he'd end up with more things to open than me and that wouldn't be very fair...we'll see what happens on Christmas morning.

I've asked for a mobile phone for my Christmas. I really hope I get one. Alyssa and Summer both have one and they can text each other whenever they want to. I'd love to be able to text my besties whenever I want to. That would be awesome!

Mum had made us some shortbread after our Christmas shopping trip, so we had that and some milk before bed.

I've LOVED today! Everything was so Christmassy, Dad said we could listen to the carol singers, Brad and I didn't fight, we had hot chocolate, Mum made us shortbread and I've spent the whole day feeling absolutely amazing!

I really needed a purple-haired day today!

"ONE DAY HER FRIEND GOT A BRAND-NEW TOY
HER HAIR WENT GREEN WITH ENVY
NO SIGN OF JOY"

Date: February 8th
Hair Colour: Green

Today's my birthday.

I woke up and mum had made Brad and me pancakes with chocolate spread, strawberries, bananas, blueberries, raspberries and THIS time she even had syrup on the table! She NEVER has syrup out in the morning because it's "just pure sugar and that's not healthy." Yeah, mum, we know! You only tell us every single day!

After breakfast, mum and dad said it was time for me to open my presents. Normally I go and get changed after breakfast, but mum said I could do that after. I asked "after what?" and she grabbed the hood on my housecoat, pulled it over my head, and gave me a big cuddle and a kiss and said "you'll see!" She's so funny sometimes!

Mum got herself a cup of tea (milk only) and dad got himself a coffee (black with 3 sweeteners unless mum makes in then he only gets 2). They were both giggling away with one another and saying how excited they were for me to get my main present. I was getting more excited too!

So, I opened all my presents and Alyssa & Summer had got together to buy me a silver necklace and bracelet set with BFF on the pendant and a BFF charm on the bracelet. It was really nice. Sparkled loads!

Brad even got me a present - a jar of farts! At least he got me something I could open, and I wouldn't expect anything less from him...

Then it came to mum and dad's stuff. I got the usual - clothes, perfume and some body sprays which smelled really nice. Mum even bought me some lip gloss which Dad wasn't too happy about, but he let me put it on. He says I can wear it about the house only but I'm sure I'll be able to wear it to school eventually.

I opened all the presents and couldn't work out why Mum and Dad were so excited - clothes, sprays and some make-up? What was so exciting about that? Don't get me wrong, I was super happy with them but I don't think it merited the giggling and the over-excited smiles they were wearing all morning. Even Brad said they were being creepy...

Then Mum got her phone and started video-chatting our grandparents. They were in their housecoats and had cups of tea too. They said "Happy Birthday" to me (sang it actually - embarrassing) and then asked me if I liked my main present? WHAT MAIN PRESENT??

What was the big deal??? What was actually going on?

Mum and Gran were chatting for aaaages then Dad came over with another present he'd stashed away. He said he just "happened to find it" but he says that every year.

It was a small box.

Could it be???

There's Mum and Dad sitting on the sofa waiting for me to open it - Dad holding his coffee, Mum on the phone to Gran and her telling Grandad "she's about to open it! Come and see her face, quickly!"
They were all really excited about this little box. I was too because of how they were acting.

I opened it...

I got...

a new phone...

You'll not believe what they did...are you ready for this???

They gave me Dad's OLD, USED phone!!! OMG!

It's got a crack running right down the screen and everything! It's so ugly! It's so worn-out looking and it's such a horrible colour. I wanted a purple one because it's my favourite colour.

I honestly thought they'd be keeping the phone as a surprise for my birthday because I didn't get it at Christmas - thought they maybe had to save up some more money or something, so I wasn't too fussed about not getting it. But noooo!

Mum, Dad, Gran and Grandad were all quietly waiting on my saying something...mum said "well….???"

Well what?! Well, thanks ever so much for giving me dads used and grubby old phone...I tried to hide my face by putting the hood on my housecoat up and sitting back on the sofa, but it was too late! Mum and Dad were very well aware of exactly how I was feeling.

Gran and Grandad didn't look very happy and Mum just said she'd phone them back in a minute. She didn't even say "bye" before hanging up and placing the phone on her lap with a heavy thump.

Mum and Dad just looked at me. Even Brad was super quiet...he kept staring at my hair. Little twerp!

Then came the lecture...I spent the next however-long listening to mum say how upset I made her because I wasn't happy with my phone. How sad she was that I was feeling jealous and how much it hurt her that I was behaving in a really ungrateful way. Eventually she went into the kitchen because she was "too upset to deal with this right now."

Dad. He just looked at me. He didn't say much. All he said was "I'm very disappointed in you, Lucy" and he left to go see mum.

How am I supposed to control how I feel?! I can't help it! I'm jealous, okay! I'm jealous of Dad because he got a new phone - it's still not even as good as Alyssa's - and I'm extra jealous of Alyssa because her phone is AMAZING! It can do EVERYTHING!!! Dad's phone is okay, MUCH better than the piece of plastic I got!!! I'd even go so far as to say Brad's present of Farts is better than the phone they got me!!

It's really not fair. Why do I have to get his old one? Why couldn't they have bought me a brand-new phone - is it really too much to ask?

I went to bed with green hair today. I thought it would be purple.

"WHEN HER LITTLE BROTHER BRAD MAKES HER REALLY, REALLY MAD HER HAIR GOES AS RED AS HER RED-HEAD DAD"

Date: March 22nd
Hair colour: Red

You know sometimes you can wake up and just feel like everything is getting in your way? Well, that was today...

My alarm didn't go off because my phone didn't charge properly and neither did anyone else's - thanks a lot, Power Cut!

Mum came running in to my room, hair all over the place, jammies twisted round her body as though she'd been caught in a tornado through the night. She yelled "Lucy! Get up!! We're late. We're ALL late!!" And then she went into Brad's room and shouted the same! Brad started crying because "he got a fright" so mum spent the next five minutes apologising and calming him down.

I could hear Dad huffing and puffing in his room while he frantically looked for his brown belt. He needed that particular belt for some reason. Mum kept saying it was on top of the washing machine, "because that's where your belts ALWAYS are because you never take them off your trousers before putting them in the machine and I have to do it before putting them in the dryer!" Mum and Dad have a system where Dad loads the washing machine and mum loads the dryer.

Apparently, Dad never seems to be able to load them properly. They both fold the washing but Mum always re-folds the towels. She likes them a particular way. It's towels, mum...towels!

While all that's going on, I get ready really quickly - so fast that I'm actually quite proud of myself - Brad hadn't even stopped crying in the time it took me...but Dad said my shirt was crushed and I'd need to change. Mum snapped at him saying there's no other clean ones because the washing hadn't been done for a couple of days and they don't have time to iron it.

So, there's Dad complaining about how "crushed I look", mum's tutting and telling him not to worry too much because "it's only one day" and while she's getting Brad dressed, Dad's making our lunch - he made me ham and cheese. I had ham and cheese yesterday and he'd promised me I'd get tuna mayo as it was a Friday and I always get tuna on a Friday. I reminded Dad it was tuna day and I was really looking forward to it but Dad said he didn't have time to make it. So, I HAD to go without...!

Brad's not being helpful either because he's running about with one shoe in his hand above his head saying he "can't find its twin", Mum's shouting to him to check under his bed, Dad's still moaning about my shirt although he did find his belt (on top of the washing machine) and I just realised I can't find my homework that's due in today...!! OH NO!!!! It's Friday! I HAVE to hand it in on a Friday!

Dad all of a sudden started yelling, "it's 10 to 9! We need to go NOW, or we'll all be late! Everyone in the car! Come on, Lucy! Forget your shirt just get in the car!!!"

I told him I couldn't find my homework - that obviously didn't help matters and he said, "see if you sorted these things the night before you go to bed, you wouldn't be in this situation in the morning. You're just going to have to go to school without it and deal with whatever the consequences are." I really wanted to say that maybe if he followed his own advice then he would know where his belt was, but I thought it would be best to not say anything that would make my morning go worse.

I got to school (looking crushed) without my homework! Great...!

There's Brad running ahead to get his friends and mum and dad didn't even get out of the car to say goodbye. I mean, I don't like them giving me a kiss at the gates or anything, but I don't mind a hug. Didn't get one today. Didn't get my tuna sandwich! Didn't get my homework and didn't get a hug! Wonderful!!!

I went over to Alyssa and Summer and before I said anything, they asked me what was wrong. I said I didn't want to talk about it.

When we went into class, we couldn't see Mrs Higgins. Where was she?

On a Friday we have to put our homework into the homework trays before we sit down. Everyone was doing this when Mr. Brown, the head teacher, walked in. He's such a tall and scary man. He just snaps at us, doesn't listen AT ALL and constantly puts his hand up to stop us from talking. He's so rude. Constantly says he wishes for the good old days when children "knew their place" whatever that means...

Oh no! I had to tell HIM that I didn't have my homework with me. He'd NEVER believe me that I hunted high and low for it and just couldn't find it! Where was Mrs Higgins??

I had no choice...I had to go and speak to HIM.

I walked over to his desk where he was now sitting (even sitting he's much taller than me) and I said, "Mr Brown, I'm really sorry but I don't have my homework today because -" and there it was...the hand! Put right in front of my face so I'd stop talking. I don't know how he does it but it works every time. Maybe he's some kind of evil wizard?

He said, "I don't want to hear any excuses, Miss Pear, no matter how you're feeling today. You will stay in class at morning interval and do it again and if you don't finish, you'll be in at lunch-time too." UGH!!! HE'S THE WORST!!! I sat down and could see in the window reflection that I had red hair. Well, that explains it, right? I'm feeling angry so the whole day is just going to be a bit rubbish!

No ironed shirt! No tuna! No homework! No Miss Higgins! Bright red hair! Great!!!

Hardly anyone spoke to me all day. Probably because my hair was bright red and everyone knows when my hair is that colour I'm feeling angry. So that actually made me feel even angrier! Why wouldn't people just come up to me and talk normally? They took one look at me and turned the other way. Even Summer and Alyssa didn't know what to say to me. I ended up saying

I had to go to the toilet during lunch and didn't go back. I just found a bench behind the school and sat there on my own thinking about how rubbish my day had been from the moment mum woke me up by yelling at me. The more I thought about it all, the redder my hair got!

When school was finished, me and Brad walked home together. He kept poking my arm and just trying to annoy me. He kept laughing at me because my hair was red and pointing to it and shouting "Everyone look! Lucy's hair is STILL RED! Ha-ha-ha-ha-ha-ha!" He's such a little snot-nosed git!!

When we got home, I just wanted to go to my room and stay there until dinner listening to music. Mum and Dad said we had to get changed right away because they had friends coming over soon. I literally didn't get to do ANYTHING I wanted to and it sucked!!

There we are, changed into our "nice clothes", sitting in the living room watching the grown-ups

talk about really, really, REALLY boring stuff.
Mortgages...whatever they were...were mentioned
and talking about how the house prices in the
area was "becoming a joke". Didn't sound like a
funny one. We weren't even allowed to have
the TV on. Dad had put some music on and it was
90's classics - REALLY OLD MUSIC!

I asked if I could go into my room and mum said
it would be rude. I didn't want to sit there
listening to them talking about boring adult stuff
and all I wanted to do was go into my room and
listen to MY music, but I wasn't allowed?! WHY
NOT!?!?!? Brad was getting to go into his room
with his friend (their son) but I had to sit there?!!!!
It's not fair!

Dinner was ready and Mum asked me to go up and
get the boys down to the table. I went upstairs
and found them both in MY ROOM and Brad was
READING MY DIARY TO HIS SILLY LITTLE FRIEND!!!!
UUUUUUGGGGGHHHH!!!!

I shouted at him to give it back! He jumped off my bed and started running around my room holding it in the air shouting "it's not fair! It's not fair! It's not fair!" to me over and over again! I chased after him trying to grab it out his hand and we ran out of my room onto the landing where mum was standing with her hands on her hips looking super cross! I tried to explain to her that Brad had been reading my diary and she put her hand up!!!! She put her hand up to stop me from speaking. Just like Mr Brown did!!!!

That silly snot-nosed little fart-breath got away with invading my privacy! Mum and Dad are ALWAYS saying we need to respect each other's privacy and just because they have friends in, Brad gets away with invading mine!!! It's not fair!!! NOT FAIR AT ALL!!!

Mum made Brad give me my diary, told me to put it back in my room and then we were all to wash our hands and get downstairs in one minute or we wouldn't be getting anything.

I left Brad and his little friend to wash their hands first because I didn't even want to be in the same room as him. Once they'd washed up, they went downstairs and I went into the bathroom. They'd used the last of the soap! OMG!!!!

I went downstairs and sat down at the table. It was curry! I love curry but I really, really hoped it was the curry WITHOUT sultanas! I hate sultanas! Dad spooned some onto my plate and there they were, sultanas.

I realised everyone had some naan on their plate but I didn't. Brad picked his up and said, "I got the last piece na-nana-nana-na". He'd managed to swipe the last bit of peshwari naan while I was washing my hands! I'd have been down in time if I hadn't gone to replace the soap that HE'D finished!

UUUUUGGGGGHHHH!

I sat there, eating my curry in silence. I didn't want to talk to anyone and thankfully, no one spoke to me.

When Mum and Dad and Brad's friends left, I asked if I could go and put on my pyjamas. Mum said I could if I wanted to but maybe I could come back out feeling a bit happier? Yeah, okay, mum! Like I can control that...

Jammies were on and I put my music on and spent the rest of the night in my room.

I didn't even want supper. I was just feeling so...mad!

I thought about the day and how everything was just rubbish and NOTHING went my way!

I went to brush my teeth and Brad had put my toothbrush under the soap! YUCK!!! I didn't realise until I put the toothbrush in my mouth, and it tasted DISGUSTING!!!! I yelled at Brad and Mum told me it could have been anyone by accident and I shouldn't be so quick to blame my brother without proof! It was DEFINITELY him! He gave me that smug look that he does when he gets away with something. He thinks they're pranks!

I went to bed feeling so angry.

Today was NOT a good day.

"LUCY DIDN'T KNOW WHERE TO LOOK AND SHE DIDN'T KNOW WHAT TO DO BECAUSE THAT MORNING SHE WOKE AND HER HAIR WAS DARK BLUE"

Date: 16th July
Hair Colour: Blue

When I woke up this morning, everything was different. The whole world looked like something I'd never seen before. The sun, even in July, didn't look so bright. My little world around me felt cold, I didn't want to get out of bed and if I am being honest, I was disappointed I even woke up. WHAT EVEN IS THAT???

I was so confused about how I felt. Things just...didn't seem right. That's the only way I can explain it. Even my dad's lame jokes didn't put a smile on my face and that's saying something. I was really worried about what colour my hair would be today? Red? No, I don't feel angry. Green? Maybe! Sometimes I feel things like this when I'm jealous. Definitely NOT purple, there is nothing happy and excited about this.

As I walked to the bathroom to check, I met my mum in the hallway, she didn't say anything, she just gave me a look, an almost scared look. Did I grow an extra head during the night? Brad even asked, "Are you ok, sis?" as I walked past his room. Why is this happening to me? I got into the bathroom and decided to look in the mirror. Where else was I going to look? WHAT?? This is new...I had no idea what to do because this morning when I woke my hair was DARK BLUE.

I stood for what felt like such a long time trying to work out what was going on. My hair was blue. I've never felt this colour before. I've never felt these FEELINGS before. What on earth is going on??

I had to go to breakfast and sit with mum and dad, blue hair and all. My mum asked why my hair was blue...like I know. I said, "Surely it's just purple and the light is making it look like this?"

"No, honey, it's blue" said my dad "and don't call me Shirley." - Yeah thanks dad - I didn't need his silly jokes. I didn't even want to go to school and whatever this "blue" feeling was I just wanted it to go away.

I don't normally wear a hoodie to school but today I HAD to. I didn't want anyone to see how I was feeling. I sat at the back of the class and didn't speak to anyone, even Mrs Higgins was worried about me. I could tell by the way she looked at me and mouthed "are you ok?" but I just nodded and put my head down so I was hidden behind the kid in front of me.

Alyssa and Summer tried to talk to me but I just didn't want to be there so why would I talk to them? Nope, my plan was to keep my hood up, sit at the back of the class and make sure no-one saw my hair.

Everything was going to plan until MR BROWN decided to come into the class. Why was he even there? He had a quiet word with Mrs Higgins and then turned to me and said, "Miss Pear, we don't wear hoods in class, kindly remove it. And Max, will you come with me?"

The entire class turned and looked at me. I could feel every single eye on me as I lifted my hands to remove my hood. What were they going to say? Will they laugh? Will they even notice? Will Summer & Alyssa still be friends with me when they see my blue, not normal, hair? I put the hood down and heard a gasp from the class. What did that mean? Were they shocked? Were they scared? Were they laughing at me?

Mrs Higgins looked at me and said, "Oh Lucy, your hair is blue, that's not too bad." I think she was trying to get the class to stop looking at me...it didn't work. I just wanted the ground to open up and swallow me. I didn't want to talk or see anyone. I just slunk into my chair and hoped people would stop looking at me. Mrs Higgins said, "Right, class, time to open your workbooks to page 36." I've never been so relieved to open a workbook before but everyone turned to face the front and stopped staring at me. Phew!

My friends were nice about it but they didn't understand it. They just kept going on and on about how happy I normally am and that I should try and "snap out of it". I just wanted to be by myself.

Lunch time came and I could feel the entire school's eyes on me. I could feel they were all talking about me, whispering what they thought my blue hair meant. I just ate my spaghetti and tried to ignore it all. Alyssa & Summer were sitting next to me chatting to each other about some nonsense they'd watched last night. I wasn't interested.

It wasn't until Alyssa started frantically tapping me on the shoulder that I paid any attention, "Lucy, Lucy, Lucy.... LUCY!"

"WHAT!?" I said

"Look, someone like you!"

What now? What is this girl talking about? Someone like me? What, sad? Face covered in Spaghetti? What is it, Alyssa?

I looked up from my empty plate. It was the new boy. I now understood why he always had his hood up. He was standing in the middle of the dinner hall and it was like a light was just shining on him.

He had it too...he had BLUE HAIR!!!

Blue hair! Just like me! Blue hair that showed exactly how he felt! I kept staring! Then I noticed something else.

He was smiling...why? I couldn't even imagine that there was someone else in the world feeling the same as me let alone have the hair that shows it. Did he feel the sadness that I felt too? I had to find out! And why was he still smiling?

I don't remember much about going over to him. I remember being very nervous and scared and feeling like the whole thing was a bit of a dream. I remember showing him my hair and I remember looking at his hair. I remember that his eyes were green, super bright green, and I remember thinking what he was saying made perfect sense.

He knew!

"Don't worry, Lucy, if your hair goes blue..." I remember him saying.

He then told me that everyone feels this way sometimes.

Really???

"We might not all have blue hair but we all have blue days. Mums and Dads all have blue days. Do you remember that day Mrs Higgins was off? She told me she was having a "Blue Day". Even though you and me can't hide our emotions, we're not alone. We're never alone and that's why I love my colour-changing hair. It lets other people see they're not alone."

I didn't speak.

"Lucy, it's important to know; It's OK to be mad, It's OK to be angry...it's OK to be sad. I know what you're feeling now is new and strange but you need to know that these feelings will fade. I promise they will. When you wake up that day, today will feel like a distant memory."

Max and I sat and spoke for most of lunch time. We spoke about the different colours that we both get and I found out that Max's hair goes white when he is scared (I wonder what mine would be?) White is pretty cool!

After school, I walked home feeling so much better. I had my blue hair flowing in the wind and it definitely helped me knowing that it was going to be ok.

When I got home, mum and dad were waiting on me. They looked worried. They sat me down and asked me what was wrong. I told them, "my hair is blue because I feel a little bit sad. I don't know why and I don't need to know why. I just feel sad...."

"...But I'll be fine," I began to say, "because it's OK, sometimes, to have a blue day."

LOOKING BACK

As you can see, I wasn't kidding about having colour-changing hair. What I didn't know though, was that my hair can actually change colour throughout the day too! I thought when I woke up my hair was a colour and that's how I'd feel that day.

How wrong was I?

Remember the time when my hair was yellow and I said that Brad looked at me weird? Well, that's because my hair changed from yellow to red and I didn't know. He made me mad, didn't he? He knew it because my hair changed to red. That's why he said "sorry" and put my tablet back. He knew I was angry with him.

It happened again when I was opening the gift from my mum and dad. I saw that it was my dad's old phone and I tried to hide the disappointment in my face but it was too late - my hair had already changed to green so mum and dad knew EXACTLY how I was feeling.

Remember when Max said his hair went white when he was scared? Mine goes silver! I noticed it when a wasp flew into my hair and I was so scared I was going to get stung. I actually saw my hair change from purple to silver.

You know those times where you're just feeling a bit grumpy for no reason but not angry? Well, my hair goes bright orange. When I'm embarrassed, it goes pink! I had no idea my hair would change into all of these colours!

Alyssa and Summer told me that once my hair went from blue back to yellow, it had all sorts of colours in it at the same time! I wish I'd seen it!

Finding this out has literally changed everything!

It's shown me that even if I wake up and feel angry, I don't have to feel that way all day. I can do something that makes me feel better.
Summer pulls the most amazing faces so when I was feeling a bit grumpy one day, I asked if she'd try to make me laugh. She did and my hair went yellow then purple! It was so cool!!

My besties know that if I'm feeling a bit orange or red then they try to make me feel better.
They ask me why I'm feeling angry and when I tell them, they understand it and just help me look at it from another point of view.

Like that time I was jealous about my phone?
They suggested that I should tell mum and dad my reasons for feeling jealous. So, I did. It was actually a lot easier than I thought it would be. I thought they'd be really upset that I'd brought it up again, but they weren't. I apologised for feeling jealous and I explained the reason was because it was cracked and I really would have

loved it in purple because it was my favourite colour. Dad showed me the crack was on a screen protector and he took it off to show the phone was actually in great condition. I was over the moon! He even had a spare screen protector in the "drawer of stuff" so put it on my phone and it looked so good! Mum ordered me a cover that was purple, so my phone looked PERFECT! I was so happy. They also told me they wished I'd just told them this because they thought I was being ungrateful and it didn't make them feel very good. They said I'm too young to get such an expensive phone for the first time and I needed to prove to them that I can take care of it.

I understood. I had to show them that I could be responsible, and I absolutely LOVE my phone. It looks so good!

I also found out that Alyssa's Mum had done the same thing. She got her mum's old phone too!! This made me feel, I don't really know...better? Sometimes I think I'm getting something and my friends are always getting something better but I've found out that a lot of what they get is second-hand as well - like Summer's school bag. She got this really lovely bag, but mum and dad said it's £38 and they don't want to spend that on a school bag. It turns out Summer's Dad got it from his brother's daughter who didn't want it anymore, so it wasn't brand-new either!

I realised that I THINK people are getting a lot more than I am and it makes me jealous. Since I started focusing on what I DO have and start appreciating it a lot more, I don't feel jealous for as long as I did. I know Summer has the most amazing house and I'd LOVE a house like hers but at least I HAVE a house and I have my own room. Summer has to share a room with her little sister, Erica and she doesn't like it because she's super messy apparently and keeps going into Summer's drawers and pulls out her clothes - she is only 2 but it makes Summer a bit angry because she likes her clothes to be neat.

As for feeling blue, it still happens from time to time. Sometimes my hair is a light blue - this is when I'm upset if I've hurt myself or watching a sad movie or something. The dark blue is the feeling I had before where everything just doesn't feel quite right. As Max said, that's normal, they're all normal! Mum even says if her hair was as special as mine it would be "blue" because she's just finished watching a film that made her cry. I wonder if she's feeling a bit jealous of my hair sometimes. She is always touching it...

My point is, no matter what feeling you're feeling in that exact moment, it will change.

You're not ALWAYS going to feel angry. Over time, the anger fades and you feel yourself again. When we're angry, we do and say things we don't mean, and it can upset people. That's not good. It's not THEIR fault we're feeling a bit angry so I've found it's always better to let people know how we're feeling and try to change it if we can.

You're not always going to feel happy. If you were ALWAYS happy, you wouldn't appreciate it as much.

You're not always going to feel sad. I've found when my hair goes dark blue that spending time by myself, listening to music in my room and drawing sketches actually help make me feel a bit better. Sometimes Mum takes me to the cinema just the two of us which helps as well. Dad taking me to the coffee shop and getting some hot chocolate and just sitting people-watching helps too. Even Brad helps by bringing me a drink if he sees my glass is empty. He is actually very sweet!

They probably wouldn't know what makes me feel happier if I didn't tell them.

Obviously, I had to re-read my diary to choose the right moments to show you that all the different feelings you might be feeling are totally normal which is why I chose the ones I did.

I really hope it helps you to understand that we're all feeling the same way and although not everyone has special hair like mine, it's good to let people you trust know how you're feeling. If it's dark blue, green or red they'll be able to help you and if it's yellow or purple, they'll share in your joy.

I've definitely seen a massive difference in how my friends help when I'm feeling a certain way because I spoke to them about it.

I hope these diary entries have helped you know that it's ok not to be ok all the time and to always talk to someone you trust and help them understand how they can help you.

Lots of Love
Your Friend
Lucy

P.S. I have left these last few pages of the diary blank for you.. Please use them. Write how you are feeling, write down what colour hair you have and how you could help yourself through any of these feelings. It helped me, and hopefully it will help you too.

Your Diary

Lisa and Chris Duke are a husband and wife team behind "Lucy's Blue Day".

Chris has experienced mental health issues throughout his life and into adulthood. He wrote "Lucy's Blue Day" to help children understand "it's ok not to be ok" and it's good to talk.

Lisa has supported Chris through his struggles, after educating herself on mental health and wants to help Chris break the stigma associated with it.

The original "Lucy's Blue Day" started as a poem intended for their eldest daughter. It was only after Lisa read it and suggested it be turned into a children's book and they started crowdfunding to pay for the illustrator that they realised the support from strangers and celebrities alike who wished for a copy too.

Dr Ranj from CBeebies' "Get Well Soon" - "it's a great little book on child mental health."
Stephen Fry - "Charming."
Lorraine Kelly - "It's such a clever, common-sense and totally relatable way to talk about mental health."

Lisa and Chris married in November 2010 and have three daughters together, Alyssa, Summer and Erica.
Chris is working on releasing his first children's novel "Archie Unplugs the Internet" at the end of 2019.

www.lucysblueday.com

30572039R00056

Printed in Great
Britain
by Amazon